Milton the Mole

CHARACTERS

Narrator

Milton Mole

Mother Mole

Millie Mole

Robert Rabbit

SETTING

A mole burrow in a meadow
Morning on a spring day

Narrator: Milton and his family were having breakfast. Suddenly, they heard a loud noise from above.

Milton: That noise again! It's so loud.

Mother: Oh, Milton, the noise is not that bad.

Millie: I like it. It sounds like a drum.

Milton: Mom, let me go try to stop it. I'll only stay aboveground a while.

Mother: The light will hurt your eyes, Milton. Be careful.

Milton: I'm tired of these bad old eyes. I wish moles didn't have such bad eyes.

Millie: I love my eyes. They're beautiful!

Mother: They are, dear. Okay, Milton. Go on. Be back soon.

Milton: I will, Mom.

Narrator: Milton dug out of his burrow. Above the burrow was a rabbit, thumping his feet as he scratched an itch.

Robert: Ah, I love a good scratch!

Milton: Oh! That sun is bright! Who are you?

Robert: I'm Robert Rabbit.

Milton: So you're making all the noise in our burrow!

Robert: I'm sorry. These big feet do make a racket. Hey, look out for that bee!

Milton: Where? I can't see it.

Robert: It's right there.

Milton: I can't see very well.
I wish I had better eyes.

Robert: I wish I had smaller feet.
What's wrong with your eyes?

Milton: It is dark where moles live. Our eyes are used to the dark. We can't see well aboveground.

Robert: So what can you do?

Milton: What do you mean?

Robert: My mom says that my big feet help me run fast. Want to see?

Milton: Sure!

Narrator: Robert ran around and around Milton. He was fast.

Milton: Wow! I wish I could do that!

Robert: I'll bet there are things you do well. Where do you live?

Milton: Here, under the ground.

Robert: How did you get up here?

Milton: I dug.

Robert: You must be a pretty good digger.

Milton: I can dig backward and forward.

Robert: How can you find things to eat down there?

Milton: I can hear a worm from pretty far away.

Robert: Hear a worm? Wow!

Milton: I can also feel food with the tip of my nose and my tail.

Robert: You sure can do a lot.

Milton: Do you really think so?

Robert: I do.

Milton: And you are a fast runner. It's a good thing you have big feet.

Robert: You're right. And you really don't need to see under the ground.

Milton: No. But I'd like to see things if I ever come up here again.

Robert: I hope you will come back. We're pals, right?

Milton: Right!

Robert: I can even help you see.

Milton: How?

Robert: Well, over there is a flower. It looks like the bright sunshine.

Milton: I can see that in my mind!

Robert: I can be your eyes when you are above the ground.

Milton: And if you ever want a worm to eat, just call on me!

Robert: Thank you. But I think I'll stick to vegetables!

Milton: I'd better get back to my hole.

Robert: See you soon. And I'll try to scratch someplace else.

Milton: Thanks! Bye!

Narrator: Milton went back down to his burrow.

Millie: Hi, Milton! What did you do up there?

Milton: I stopped the noise and made a friend.

Mother: You seem happy.

Milton: I am. Millie was right.

Millie: I was?

Mother: Right about what?

Milton: Millie said that her eyes are beautiful. My eyes are beautiful, too, even if they don't see very well.

Mother: That's true!

Milton: Moles can do many things well. Who needs to see in a dark burrow? I can dig and hear and feel!

Millie: I can sing!

Mother: Sing us a song, Millie.

Millie: I love being a mole, a mole in a hole.

Millie and **Milton:** Oh, a mole in a hole, that's me!

The End